FLASHING
FIRE ENGINES

For Renée, Eric, Cornelia and Saskia – T.M.

**The Publisher thanks the London Fire Brigade Headquarters and
the New York City Fire Department Public Information Office
for their kind assistance in the development of this book.**

KINGFISHER

First published by Kingfisher 1998
This edition published by Kingfisher 2007
an imprint of Macmillan Children's Books
a division of Macmillan Publishers Limited
20 New Wharf Road, London N1 9RR
Basingstoke and Oxford
Associated companies throughout the world
www.panmacmillan.com

ISBN: 978-0-7534-1489-7

Text copyright © Tony Mitton 1998 Illustrations copyright © Ant Parker 1998
The moral right of the author and illustrator has been asserted.

3 5 7 9 10 8 6 4 2

A CIP catalogue record for this book is available from the British Library.

Printed in China

FLASHING FIRE ENGINES

Tony Mitton and Ant Parker

KINGFISHER

Big, bold fire engines, waiting day and night,

ready for a rescue or a blazing fire to fight.

As soon as there's a fire alarm,
the engine starts to roar.

The firefighters jump aboard –
it rumbles out the door.

Watch the engine speeding, on its daring dash,

Hear its siren screaming. See its bright lights flash.

In helmets, fireproof coats and trousers, boots so big and strong,

the crew are dressed and ready
as the engine zooms along.

When the engine finds the fire,
it quickly pulls up near.

The crew jump out, unroll the hose
and get out all the gear.

The hose has got a nozzle
that shoots a jet of spray.
It squirts right at the blazing flames
and sizzles them away.

The water tank is empty soon,
so where can more be found?
The engine's pump can pull it up
from pipes below the ground.

The fire is hot and roaring.
It makes a lot of smoke.

The firefighters put on masks,
otherwise they'd choke.

The ladder rises upward. It reaches for the sky.
A fire engine's ladder stretches up so very high!

Sometimes there's a platform, right up at the top.
It waits beside the window. Then into it you hop.

At last the fire's extinguished.
The flames are all put out.

plop!

plop!

Lower the ladder. Roll the hose.
"Hooray!" the fire crew shout.

Back inside the station,
the crew can take a break.

But the fire engine's ready
and it's waiting wide-awake.

Fire Engine bits

helmet

this is a hard hat that protects the firefighter's head

siren

this makes a loud noise to tell people to move out of the way and let the fire engine pass

fireproof coats and trousers

these are made from special material that does not burn easily and protects firefighters from the fire

masks and tank

we cannot breathe in smoky air so firefighters carry clean air in **tanks** on their backs and this flows into their **masks**

water tank

this is inside the middle of the fire engine and holds water to fight the fire – some fire engines carry foam, too

pump

this sucks water from the tank and pushes it out through tubes called **hoses** – it also gets water from underground through big taps in the street called **hydrants**

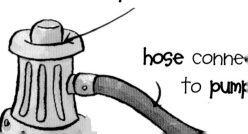

hose conne... to **pump**